Time Travel
Winnie

LAURA OWEN & KORKY PAUL

OXFORD
UNIVERSITY PRESS

Helping your child to read

Before they start

* ★ Talk about the back cover blurb. What adventures does your child think Winnie might have when she goes back in time?
* ★ Which of the two stories does your child think sounds most interesting, and why?

During reading

* ★ Let your child read at their own pace – don't worry if it's slow. They could read silently, or read to you out loud.
* ★ Help them to work out words they don't know by saying each sound out loud and then blending them to say the word, e.g. *p-o-ng-y*, *pongy*.
* ★ If your child still struggles with a word, just tell them the word and move on.
* ★ Give them lots of praise for good reading!

After reading

* ★ Look at page 48 for some fun activities.

Contents

Winnie's Time Machine ... 5

Winnie Spells Trouble ... 27

OXFORD
UNIVERSITY PRESS

Great Clarendon Street, Oxford OX2 6DP
Oxford University Press is a department of the University of Oxford.
It furthers the University's objective of excellence in research, scholarship,
and education by publishing worldwide. Oxford is a registered trade mark
of Oxford University Press in the UK and in certain other countries

Text © Oxford University Press
Illustrations © Korky Paul

The characters in this work are the original creation of Valerie Thomas
who retains copyright in the characters.

"Winnie's Time Machine" was first published in *Spooky Winnie* in 2013
"Winnie Spells Trouble" was first published in *Winnie Spells Trouble* in 2014
This edition published 2019

The moral rights of the author/illustrator have been asserted

Database right Oxford University Press (maker)

British Library Cataloguing in Publication Data

Data available

ISBN: 978-0-19-276916-9

1 3 5 7 9 10 8 6 4 2

Printed in China

Paper used in the production of this book is a natural,
recyclable product made from wood grown in sustainable forests.
The manufacturing process conforms to the environmental
regulations of the country of origin.

Acknowledgements
With thanks to Catherine Baker for editorial support

Winnie's Time Machine

⭐ Chapter ⭐ One

Winnie's garden was a bit of a mess. "That flower bed looks as if something big has sat on it," she said. "But just wait till I plant my lovely new lolly lily plant. It'll give me fresh lollies all summer long!"

Winnie had just planted the lolly lily when she heard a strange noise.

Crash! Ting! Ping!

"Oh dear, oh drat!" said a voice.

"That sounds like Jerry the giant next door," said Winnie to Wilbur. "Come on. Let's see what he's doing."

Winnie and Wilbur jumped over Jerry's high fence. They went all the way round to his giant front door, and opened it. Out came a big wave of soapy water.

Sploosh!

Out swept Scruff the dog on a frothy wave of water.

"What in the witchy world is going on here?" said Winnie.

"It's my washing machine," said Jerry, wading through a soggy pile of clothes. "I was just washing my underwear when my machine started banging."

Jerry held up a giant mallet. "I couldn't find my hammer, so I tried mending it with this," he said. "But I think I've just made things worse!"

"I'll do your washing in my machine if you like," said Winnie.

"Oh, thanks, Winnie!" said Jerry.

But soon, Winnie found out there was a problem. She stuffed all of Jerry's huge pongy socks into her washing machine. "Drat!" she said. "Now the machine is completely full! It'll take forever to do all Jerry's giant washing!"

Squirt-slosh-churn-rattle-sigh-clunk! went the washing machine.

Next, Winnie washed Jerry's overalls. When she took them out of the machine she found something large in the pocket.

"It's his hammer!" Winnie said. "No wonder the machine was banging."

It was hard work doing the washing – but even harder work hanging it up to dry. Wilbur helped Winnie to hang a gigantic shirt on her washing line. But the sleeves were so long that they dangled in the dirt.

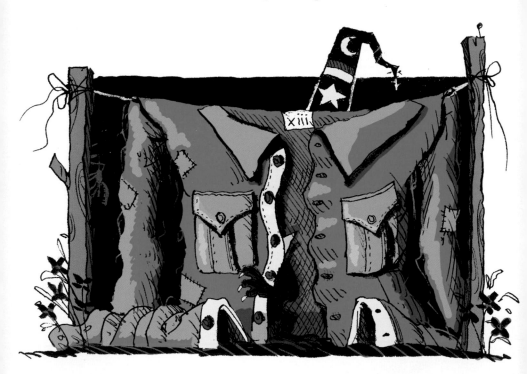

And the shirt was so huge and heavy that
the whole washing line fell down! **Twang!**

"Oh, wobbling wombats!" said Winnie.
"Now all the washing is dirty again! Jerry!"
she yelled. "You'll have to put up a new
washing line for us!"

★ Chapter Two ★

Jerry tied a washing line between two giant trees. Then Winnie and Wilbur flew up on the broom to hang up the washing.

"Mee-hee-hee-ow!" laughed Wilbur when he saw Jerry's fancy pants.

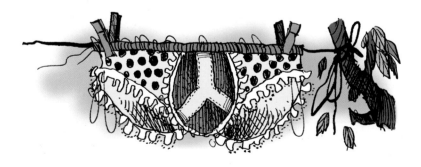

"There!" said Winnie at last. "All done!"

Flash! Thunder! Rumble!

"Oh, no!" said Winnie. "Please don't rain!" But a storm had started. It poured with rain.

15

"How are we going to get the washing dry now?" said Winnie. "Poor Jerry is shivering with cold. He needs some clothes and none of mine would fit him – even if he wanted to borrow a purple dress."

Winnie and Jerry were just wondering what to do, when Wilbur pointed at the clock.

"Meeow!" he said. It was time for his favourite television programme, *Mice in the Attic*. But the clock made Winnie think of something else.

"You've given me a great idea, Wilbur!" she said. "We'll make a machine to turn the time back! We'll go back to *before* Jerry broke his washing machine. That'll solve all the problems!"

So Winnie and Wilbur and Jerry made a big pile of chairs and levers and knobs and buttons. Then Winnie added the clock.

"Stand back!" said Winnie, waving her wand. "**Abracadabra!**"

"Come on," said Winnie. "All aboard the time machine!" Winnie and Wilbur put on cauldrons as crash helmets and climbed into the machine. Jerry squeezed in, too.

18

"Right," said Winnie. "Set the time machine for eight o'clock this morning."

Wilbur was just setting the clock when . . .

A flash of lightning from the storm outside made them all jump. Wilbur's paw slipped and he set the clock to the wrong time!

ZOOM! SHAKE! RATTLE AND ROLL!

Suddenly, they were all speeding through time and space.

★ Chapter ★
Three

"W-w-w-where and w-w-w-when are we
going, I w-w-w-wonder?" said Winnie,
holding on tight.

"N-n-n-no idea!" said Jerry. **Bump!** They
landed in a damp, dark cave.

"Meeow!" Wilbur pointed to where a fire
was burning at the cave entrance.

"Good-good-good," said Winnie and her echo. "There must be somebody here-here-here."

But they couldn't see anybody, just a drawing on the cave wall.

"Whoever lives here has a cat," said Winnie. "And a dog. So they must be ever so friendly!"

"They've got giant animals, too!" said Jerry, picking up some huge bones.

Just then they saw somebody at the cave entrance.

"Er, I think it's time to leave," said Jerry, because the person at the cave entrance didn't look very friendly at all. She was holding a spear!

"Oggle-bog-flog!" shouted the cave woman. The ground started to shake.

The very next moment, a huge mammoth
ran by.

"It really is time to go home!" said Winnie.
"Come on, you two. Hold tight!" She waved
her wand. "**Abracadabra!**"

Whirl-swirl-twirl-clatter-clatter.

23

They landed back in Winnie's kitchen.

"We've got home safe and sound!" said
Winnie. "But what on earth was that
clattering noise?"

"It was these huge bones," said Jerry.
"They came back with me."

"Hmm, I wonder what kind of animal
they belonged to?" said Winnie. "Let's see."
She waved her wand. "**Abracadabra!**"

The bones wiggled and jiggled up into
the air. When they fell into place they made
a very odd-looking animal.

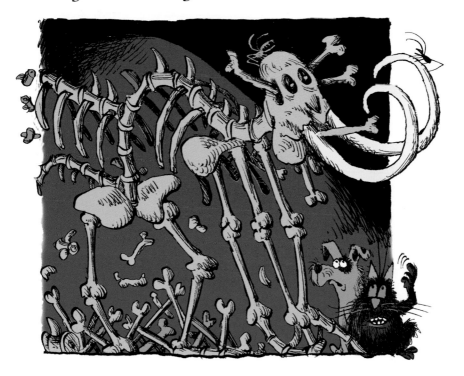

"Oooh! I don't think five legs and two
tails can be right, can it?" said Winnie. She
waved her wand again. "**Abracadabra!**"

When the bones settled this time, the
skeleton looked a bit like a mammoth.

Winnie decided it would make a perfect clothes rack. Jerry's clothes were dry in no time at all.

Later on, Winnie put the mammoth skeleton in the garden. The lolly lily plant grew all over it, and it looked lovely!

Winnie
Spells
Trouble

28

⭐ Chapter ⭐ One

"Up you get, Wilbur!" said Winnie, jabbing
Wilbur with her wand.

"Meeow!" scowled Wilbur.

"Hurry up!" said Winnie. "Mrs Parmar
has just phoned to say that one of the
teachers has fallen over and had to go to
hospital. We have to help Mrs Parmar take
the children to the museum."

Winnie and Wilbur got to school just in time for the trip. The children all walked to the museum in pairs, holding hands.

"I'll hold hands with you, Mrs Parmar," said Winnie.

"You will not!" said Mrs Parmar, crossing her arms. So Winnie held paws with Wilbur instead.

The museum was full of strange things with labels and musty smells.

"We have to learn about the Egyptians," said Mrs Parmar. She led everyone into a room full of mummies. "Winnie," said Mrs Parmar, "please read out the label on that stone coffin. That's a sar-coff-a-gus. Listen to Winnie, children!"

Just as Winnie began to read, she noticed a boy had started jigging up and down, looking red in the face. "Oooh-oooh-oooh!"

"What is it, Henry?" asked Mrs Parmar.

"I need to go to the loo-oo-oo!" said Henry. "I really, really do-oo-oo!"

"Look, the loos are over there," Winnie said, pointing to two doors with pictures on them.

"Come on, Henry," said Mrs Parmar. "Winnie, you are to stay here with the other children, and *don't go anywhere!*"

"Look!" said a girl called Daisy. "There's an Egyptian cat, all wrapped in bandages! Let's wrap up Wilbur!"

Wilbur went to hide behind Winnie.

Winnie was looking at the sarcophagus.
It had lots of little pictures of birds and
hands and beetles and triangles. "That's
writing in pictures!" said Winnie.

"What does it say, then?" asked one of
the children.

"Well," said Winnie. She pointed her
wand at one little picture, and . . .

Kerpooof!

The museum seemed to melt and swirl into a rushing wind that turned into a whirl of sand and heat.

"Wilburrr!" Winnie clutched Wilbur's paw as they spun into the time-changing magic. The children clutched each other's hands, too, and one held on to Wilbur's tail. The magic took them back . . . back . . . to ancient Egypt!

⭐ Chapter ⭐ Two

They landed in a flat desert. "Phew, it's as hot as a dragon's hanky when it has blown its nose!" said Winnie.

"Meeow!" said Wilbur, pointing at Winnie. She suddenly looked like an Egyptian queen.

Wilbur looked different, too. "You're as posh as a poodle, Wilbur!" said Winnie.

All the children were dressed as Egyptians.

Winnie sat on a throne. One of the children fanned her, and the others played twangy music.

"Oooh, I like this," said Winnie. "Thank you, children!"

Wilbur was happy, too. The children
brought him treats to eat, and they knelt
down in front of him.

"Oooh, Wilbur, they're worshipping you!"
laughed Winnie.

But Wilbur gave Winnie a powerful look,
and Winnie quickly stopped laughing.

"Er, I meant to call you Your Cattiness,
Wilbur the Great," she said.

"Meeow," nodded Wilbur.

Just then Winnie noticed that a man with
a whip was shouting at the children. The poor
children were trying to pull a huge stone along
with ropes. They were sweating and panting.
"Hurry up," the man yelled. "We need to
finish the pyramid before it gets dark."

"Hey!" shouted Winnie to the man. "Leave
those children alone! Don't be such a bully!"
But the man took no notice.

"Oh, piffling pyramids!" said Winnie. "I must get the children back to the museum before Mrs Parmar notices we've gone. But that man won't let them go until they've built the pyramid!" Winnie thought for a moment, then she had an idea. She waved her wand. "**Abracadabra!**"

✫ Chapter ✫
Three

Suddenly, all the children were super strong.
They picked up the huge stones, ran to the
half-built pyramid and finished building it
in no time. The man with the whip just stood
with his mouth open.

"Come along, children, you're all free!"
shouted Winnie. "Now we just need to
find Wilbur."

But Wilbur didn't want to leave.

"Meeow," said Wilbur, shaking his head.
He liked being worshipped!

"I'll serve you treats when we get home,"
said Winnie. Wilbur gave her a look.

"I might even kneel down," said Winnie. Wilbur didn't see her fingers crossed behind her back.

"Now, everybody hold hands and paws!" said Winnie loudly. She waved her wand in the air. "**Abracadabra!**"

Suddenly, they all landed back in the
museum, right next to Mrs Parmar.

"Winnie the Witch, I told you not to go
anywhere!" said Mrs Parmar.

But then some of the children started
playing the ancient Egyptian instruments
they had brought back. Twangy music filled
the museum. The music started to work like
magic. At once, Mrs Parmar began walking
like an ancient Egyptian.

"Walk like me!" said Mrs Parmar. So they all walked like Egyptians, all the way back to school.

The teacher was back from hospital, wrapped in bandages. He looked just like a mummy.

When they got home, Winnie gave
Wilbur some nice crunchy beetles to eat.
Then he fell asleep, dreaming of mice and
camels and pyramids, and being worshipped
by Winnie. Purrrr!

After reading activities

Quick quiz

See how fast you can answer these questions! Look back at the stories if you can't remember.

1) In "Winnie's Time Machine", what kind of plant does Winnie plant in her garden?
2) In "Winnie's Time Machine", what does Jerry bring back with him from the past?
3) In "Winnie Spells Trouble", why doesn't Wilbur want to leave ancient Egypt?

1) a lolly lily plant; 2) a mammoth skeleton; 3) he's having too much fun being worshipped

Talk about it!

★ If you could go back in time to any point in history, where would you go? Why?
★ Would you like to go on a school trip with Winnie the Witch? What kinds of things might happen?